FRANKIE FROG
and the
THROATY CROAKERS

FREYA HARTAS

Albert Whitman & Company
Chicago, Illinois

For my dearest Gramps, the most splendid frog of all

Library of Congress Cataloging-in-Publication data is on file with the publisher.

Text and illustrations copyright © 2019 by Freya Hartas
First published in the United States of America
in 2019 by Albert Whitman & Company
ISBN 978-0-8075-2543-2

Printed in China
10 9 8 7 6 5 4 3 2 1 WKT 22 21 20 19 18

Design by Morgan Beck

For more information about Albert Whitman & Company,
visit our website at www.albertwhitman.com.

100 Years of Albert Whitman & Company
Celebrate with us in 2019!

There comes a time in every young frog's life when he or she lets out their very first CROAK!

It is a very important occasion, no matter what that little frog is doing.

Whether they are
eating breakfast,

learning math
at school,

hopping over the
water lilies,

or even sitting
on the toilet!

Everybody has to stop what they're doing and celebrate that little frog's first croak.

But for one little frog, a frog called Frankie,
that first croak never came.

At first his parents said, "Don't worry Frankie, your croak will come. You just have to be patient."

But years passed and he grew from a little frog into a big frog with not even the teeniest of croaks. He exercised his throat muscles, gargled with pond water, and listened to all the great croakers from froggy history, but nothing worked.

Other frogs could croak, and the birds could twitter, and the crickets could chirrup, and the ducks could quack. It seemed everyone in the pond had a song of their own. Everyone but Frankie.

He would never enter the annual Croak Competition
or join in at croak o'clock, when all the frogs gathered
together for an evening serenade of croaking.

One night Frankie was wishing for a croak when he heard a new sound from far across the pond. It was sweet and pure and quite unlike any croak he had heard before.

The sound buzzed
through the bulrushes

and fluttered
over the flowers.

It jingled and jangled
and tingled and tangled.

Frankie followed
the sound to a clearing in the
woods, where a beautiful princess sat
watching four joyful humans playing
four strange objects. As they played, music
sounded. "This must be a music machine,"
thought Frankie. "The secret to
that beautiful sound!"

"They are making music without croaking," Frankie thought. "Maybe I can too!"

Frankie jumped for joy! He hipped and hopped and flipped and flopped!

Then he silently thanked the princess and the players and ran back home as fast as he could.

Luckily frogs are very good at making things, and he had his own music machine ready before dawn. "I think I'll call you Banjo," he thought to himself, then let out a tiny froggy yawn.

He picked up the machine just as the morning song of the pond began.

The first sound that Frankie made with Banjo was horrible.

The second sound was pretty horrible too. But after the eighty-eighth sound, it actually sounded pretty good...

and by the two
hundredth sound,
it sounded amazing!

Felicity, Furgis, and Fintan heard the beautiful
sound and were surprised to see who was making it.
"It's Frankie, the frog who can't croak!" they said.
"But what a lovely sound he is making now!"

He helped them make
three music machines:

CLANG!
CLANG!

VZZSSHHH
VZZSSHHH

Twang

one that honked,

HONK!

one that bashed,

BANG

and one that plucked.

Screeeech!

At first they sounded pretty terrible together, but
after lots of honking, bashing, and plucking, and a bit
of help from Frankie himself, they actually sounded
good. In fact, better than good, they sounded fantastic!

The frogs who had gathered together for croak o'clock lifted their froggy ears to the most beautiful sound they had ever heard.

They set off to find out where it was coming from.

"Ladies and Gentlefrogs, introducing Frankie Frog and the Throaty Croakers!" Felicity Frog croaked.

Frankie grinned, and the band played all evening and way after froggy bedtime.

Frankie, Felicity, Furgis, and Fintan got better and better, and this year, when the annual Croak Competition came around, Frankie wanted to be a part of it.

But the three Croak Competition judges shook their heads. "Only croaking frogs can enter the Croak Competition," they said. Felicity, Furgis, and Fintan looked at Frankie sadly, but Frankie had another brilliant idea!

If he'd made a human machine like Banjo, surely he could make a froggy machine too!

Frankie set off with his friends to collect all things froggy. Felicity gathered the freshest pond water, Furgis plucked the loveliest lily pad, and Fintan found the biggest, bushiest bulrush.

Frankie added some nice green water reeds and made the first ever croaking machine!

At first it sounded very strange, the second time it
sounded slightly better, and by the third it sounded fabulous!

When the crowds discovered Frankie and the Throaty Croakers were playing, they threw up a cheer! And in the midst of all the music, Frankie introduced his new croaking machine and won the whole competition. The Throaty Croakers cheered loudest of all.

All the frogs of the pond clapped and cheered and jumped for joy and Frankie made a big, happy, throaty CROAK!

Other frogs could croak, and the birds could twitter, and the crickets could chirrup, and the ducks could quack. Everyone in the pond had a song of their own—including Frankie.